I THE GUY
HISTORIAN'S
JOURNAL

The Bryan Museum
the Romance of The West

IWRITE.ORG

Funded by the generosity of the Ippolito Charitable
Foundation and the Texas Historical Foundation.

IPPOLITO
CHARITABLE FOUNDATION

TEXAS
HISTORICAL FOUNDATION
EST. 1954

HI!

I'm "i" The Guy!
and who are you?

That's where your name goes.

WARNING!

This is not a textbook. This historian's journal will take you on adventures and inspire you to write your own stories! If you ever get bored, remember I'm here to help.

Your friend,

¡ The GUY

"i" The Guy here! If you're reading this, you must be interested in adventures and stories, just like me. It's important to write things down in a journal, like this one. That way your history is not lost. You are literally living out history as we speak!

History changes the world! How do you want people to remember you?

Take the Spanish explorer Álvar Núñez Cabeza de Vaca for example. Yeah try saying that name fast five times. This guy's journal changed history ... right here in Texas! Cabeza de Vaca traveled from Spain to present day Texas. He and his men washed ashore on Galveston Island and were captured by the natives. For eight years they traveled together, and he eventually became a healer and earned their trust. He kept a journal and wrote about his experiences as a slave.

DID YOU KNOW? *Cabeza de Vaca walked around for six years without shoes!*

What could be something
important that Cabeza
de Vaca wrote about in
his journal?

You are already on a journey of collecting primary research and inspiration! (On the next page I'll tell you the difference between primary and secondary research.) Museums are full of primary research, like artifacts, journals and historical documents. If I were you, I'd take this journal to a Texas History museum to collect more inspiration for your writing!

"i" The Guy's Favorite Texas History Museums

- The Bryan Museum in Galveston
- The Museum of History in El Paso
- The Bullock in Austin
- National Cowgirl Museum and Hall of Fame in Fort Worth
- The Witte in San Antonio

Fun Fact: Texas is the only state that used to be its own country. Now that is **HUGE!**

Research:

PRIMARY: Something or someone who has lived through history and provides information.
- Historical and Legal Documents
- Eyewitness Accounts
- Interviews and Surveys
- Art Objects

LAND GRANT ➤

Write down a primary resource you found at a museum.

_____

SECONDARY: Secondary sources describe and summarize primary sources. The author of the source did not personally experience it.
- Articles in Newspapers or Popular Magazines
- Book or Movie Review
- Articles that Discuss Someone Else's Original Research

My Favorite Fun Facts at the Museum

_____

_____

_____

_____

_____

_____

"i" The Guy's Favorite Fun Facts At The Museum

1. Cabeza de Vaca wrote in a journal too!

2. Texas used to be its own country for only ten years - Republic of Texas

How did your research go? Most writers have to research before they write stories. Write me a story about your day at the museum. Be sure to include examples of things you got to see and what you learned.

Today I got to...

_____

_____

_____

_____

_____

_____

_____

_____

_____

_____

_____

_____

Texas has some great stories! Most are action adventures. All stories have a few things in common.

MAIN CHARACTER,

PROBLEM and *SOLUTION*

Let's start with the most important part of all stories... **THE MAIN CHARACTER!** Check out some of my favorite main characters found in the adventures of Texas History starting on the next page.

Jane Hughs

Jane Hughs was given a land grant from Stephen F. Austin to come and settle in Texas. She was considered to be a part of the Old 300 - the first families of settlers who came to colonize land in Texas. For a woman to receive a land grant was almost unheard of during this time in history.

DID YOU KNOW? *Jane Hughs' and all land grants were written in Spanish.*

Stephen F. Austin

When Moses Austin died, his son, Stephen F. Austin, continued the work of his father and received permission from the government, following the Mexican War of Independence (1810-1821), to bring 300 Anglo families to settle his colony in Texas. He organized trade with the United States. Over the next decade and a half, he received empresario grants and worked together with the new Mexican government, until Santa Anna took control as a dictator. Stephen F. Austin was put in prison for a year in a half for holding conventions to discuss the problems they were having with the Mexican government.

DID YOU KNOW? *Stephen F. Austin is called, The Father of Texas.*

Empresario Grants: After Mexican independence in 1821, the Mexican government contracted land agents to aid the settlement of Texas.

Santa Anna

When Antonio López de Santa Anna came to power in Mexico as president, he threw out the Constitution of 1824. This upset many of the colonists in Texas. Combined with other grievances, many became determined to create an independent Texas. In 1835, the Consultation, a provisional Texas government, formed to head a new separate state. Santa Anna marched a large Mexican Army across the Rio Grande into Texas. He annihilated the Texians at the Alamo and ordered the entire captured army at Goliad to be executed. He pursued Sam Houston's Texian army, prompting the *Runaway Scrape* across Texas to safety along the Louisiana border. Santa Anna's army caught up with Houston, and on April 21, 1836, Houston defeated the Mexican army at the Battle of San Jacinto, securing Texas's independence from Mexico.

Sam Houston

After General Sam Houston led the Texas army to victory at the Battle of San Jacinto, the Republic of Texas operated as a sovereign nation for the next decade. Sam Houston was elected the first president, and the basics of a nation was created: a postal system, a standing army, a navy, money and legislatures. The Republic allowed colonization to continue, prompting a group of German nobles to purchase a large area of land and settle families near present-day Fredericksburg, Texas. The Republic was annexed by the United States in 1845.

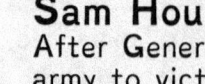

DID YOU KNOW? *Sam Houston joined a tribe of Cherokee Indians when he was 16 years old. His Cherokee name was Colonneh, which meant Raven.*

Quanah Parker

Quanah was born in 1845 and his name meant *smell* or *odor*. Quanah was the son of Peta Nocona, a Comanche chief, and Cynthia Ann Parker, an American. He became a Comanche leader, the last chief of the Quahada Comanche Indians. As chief, he started an alliance of multiple tribes against the buffalo hunters and Anglo expansion in northwest Texas. After months of fighting Parker, the tribes surrendered to the army and moved to the Kiowa-Comanche reservation in southwestern Oklahoma. Quanah Parker became the spokesman and peacetime leader of Native Americans in reservations. He died Feb 23, 1911 in Cache, Oklahoma.

Vivian White

Vivian White was a famous cowgirl on the rodeo circuit during the first half of the 20th century. Born in 1913, Vivian White grew up on her family farm in Oklahoma and competed in her first rodeo at the age of fourteen. After winning her first World Champion's title in saddle bronc riding in 1937 at Madison Square Garden, she proceeded to win that title again in 1941, which happened to be the last year that women were allowed to compete in the *men's circuit*. Following World War II, women rodeo competitors created an *all-girl circuit,* named the Girl's Rodeo Association. Vivian White won that organization's saddle bronc world title in 1949, after which she retired from the circuit.

Bose Ikard

Bose Ikard, born a slave in Mississippi in the 1840's, came to Texas as a child with the family of his owner, Dr. Milton L. Ikard. In 1866, he joined the Goodnight-Loving Trail and became one of Charles Goodnight's best cowboys. He was one of the first African Americans to be inducted into the Hall of Great Westerners by the National Cowboy Museum. He died in 1929, and on Ikard's monument, Goodnight had the following words inscribed: "Served with me four years on the Goodnight-Loving Trail, never shirked duty or disobeyed an order, rode with me in many stampedes, participated in three engagements with Comanches, splendid behavior."

"i" The Guy's Extra Brainstorming Page!

Did any of those real characters from Texas History interest you? Write down a few things that you thought were cool from the previous pages.

When you start to study the lives of some of the people I mentioned on the last few pages, you realize that many of them encountered some kind of problem. These people solved their problems, but at times their problems led to even bigger problems!

Let's talk about the next important thing to include in a story ... the **character's problem**. I like solving problems!

Throughout the history of Texas, there were a lot of problems and conflicts that people had to fix. That's why we have a constitution and rules to follow in Texas and in America.

Let's talk about some of Texas' problems before it became part of the United States in 1845.

PROBLEMS

Texas had some issues!

Even though Texas won its freedom from Mexico, President Sam Houston and the Texans constantly worried about future attacks from the Mexicans.

Many people living in the Republic of Texas thought it would be safer to become part of the United States, but the Republic of Texas had a lot of unpaid debt caused from the war. The United States did not want to take on the extra debt and the United States didn't like the idea of adding one more slave state to the Union.

Texas agriculture relied on enslaved labor.

Mexico still wanted to take Texas back. Some of the leaders inside the United States were worried that if Texas became part of the United States, Mexico would start a war with the U.S.

Do you know where we got the phrase, **SIX FLAGS OVER TEXAS?**

Texas has had six official flags!

1500s – Spanish Flag
The Spanish Flag represents the first Spanish explorers to arrive in what is now Texas.

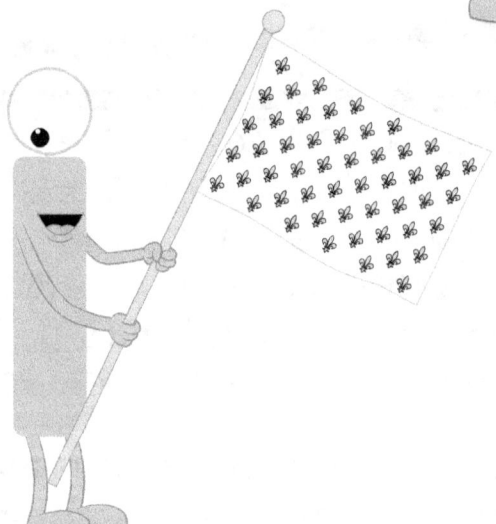

1685 – French Flag The French Flag flew over Texas when Robert de la Salle claimed the land.

1800s – Mexico Flag
The Mexican Flag flew over Texas in the early 1800s.

1839 – Republic of Texas Flag
The Republic of Texas flag represented Texas as its own country, and later became the current state flag.

1845 – United States of America Flag
When Texas became the 28th state, the United States flag flew over Texas.

1861 – Confederate States Flag
When Texas seceded from the Union to join the Confederacy, the Confederate States flag flew over Texas.

1870 – United States of America Flag
The stars and stripes flew over Texas again when it joined back with the Union. It has been flying ever since.

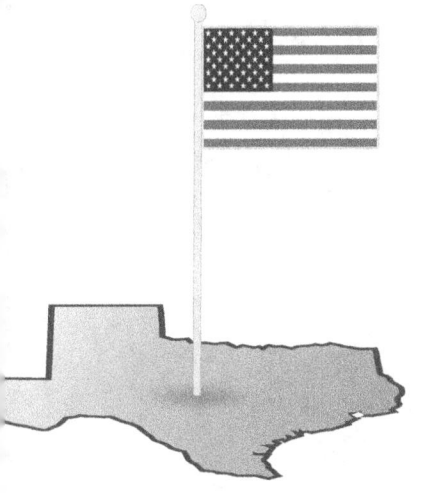

You know there were lots of problems that continued to emerge in Texas. I found a letter from my Great Grandpa, Old Man "i", who lived in Texas, to his friend who lived in the north. It's full of even more problems!

Read out loud in an old man's voice.

December 29, 1860

Dear Marshal,

I'm about to pull out my eyeball if everyone can't just get along. You know my neighbor, Alfred Nosehole, owns a big plantation here in Texas. He's afraid ole Abe Lincoln is going to pass a law and force him to free his slaves. I get that Alfred depends on them to work on the farm, so he can make money, but these people are humans too. It's just not right. Did you hear that South Carolina just seceded from the United States? There is talk that us folks in Texas are about to separate too. They're going to call the states that separate the Confederate States of America. It just sounds like everyone is scared, angry and confused if you ask me. It's bad enough the Comanche Indians have a problem with us too. Land and that big old buffalo is like gold to everyone here. If we all aren't careful, we're going to start a Civil War.

Your friend, Old Man

PUTTING YOURSELF IN A CHARACTER'S SHOES

As you see, not everyone in the south supported slavery. What do you think Marshal, who lived in the north back in the 1860s, would have written back to my Great Grandfather? Go ahead and give it a try. Pretend to be Marshal. Be sure to predict what Marshal thinks might happen next. Can Marshal predict the future?

Dear Old Man "i",

If you and Marshal agreed with my Great Grandfather regarding the start of the Civil War over slavery, you were right. Check out what happened next.

The Civil War started on April 12, 1861 between the Northern and Southern States.

SOUTH	NORTH
Confederate General: General Robert E. Lee	Union General: Ulysses S. Grant

Why were they fighting?

_____

_____

_____

_____

_____

The Infantry: Texans who fought on foot.	The Cavalry: Texans who fought on horseback.	The Artillery: Texans who fired the big cannons.

DID YOU KNOW?: Some Texans fought for the Union.

Women worked as nurses to the injured soldiers. They also made uniforms, tents, blankets, bandages, and tended to the homefront.

On October 1862, the Union captured the port at Galveston Harbor. The Confederacy recaptured the fort on January 1, 1863.

The Confederacy surrendered on April 9, 1865.

How long did the war last?

How did this war change America?

Who was the president of the United States in 1865?

Hint: There were 2 presidents that year.

Flip to page 121 to read
Abraham Lincoln's Emancipation Proclamation

LIFE ON THE TEXAS RANGE

Now that the Civil War is over, I've got a few fun facts to share with you to get you ready for life out on the Texas Range. I'll give you a clue, it's got a lot to do with **COWS!**

 After the Civil War, Texas was broke!

 Texas had **A LOT** of cows and ranchers.

 Texas had lots of cowboys to round up the cows.

 Cows taste good!

 Texans drove the herds north to sell the beef at markets.

 Cows got to travel on the railroads.

The Goodnight-Loving Trail

Charles Goodnight was a famous cattle rancher and cowboy. He and Oliver Loving were known for the cattle trail that they blazed in 1866 from Texas all the way to New Mexico, Colorado and Wyoming. The trail was named The Goodnight-Loving Trail. Eventually the cattle driving business came to an end. Check out some of the problems caused by the cattle drives.

PROBLEMS

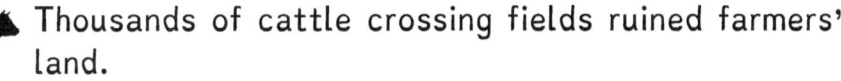 Thousands of cattle crossing fields ruined farmers' land.

 Texas fever: a disease carried by cattle on the trails.

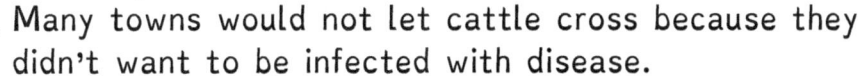 Many towns would not let cattle cross because they didn't want to be infected with disease.

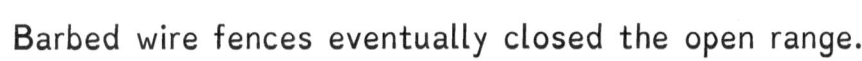 Barbed wire fences eventually closed the open range.

New railroads were built, which made the large drives unnecessary and decreased the cowboy industry.

Do you know the name of the largest cattle ranch in the United States today? It was nearly 825,000 acres big! Want to see a cool map of the cattle drive trails? Turn to page 123.

Answer: The King Ranch in Kingsville, started in 1852.

List a few problems you think a cowboy might have had during the cattle drives.
I'll get you started. You should check out some of the cowboy gear on page 125.

Dust storms

Cowboys wore bandanas over their nose and mouth, so they wouldn't breathe in dirt from the dust storms.

THE RAILROADS!!!

Did you know the very first railroads in Texas were near the **Gulf Coast** in the early 1800s? During the 19th century, hundreds of thousands of people had moved to Texas. By the early 1900s, Texas had more railroads than any other state. Eventually the population increased to over two million people.

How did **Railroads** help Texas become such a great state? Write about it. I'll start you off.

The railroads helped Texas...

I found another letter to my Great Grandfather's friend, Marshal. It was dated only a year before he died. I wish people today wrote more letters. I think they are kind of cool to go back and read. It tells me a lot about my grandparents' history. It sounds like he made a lot of money off oil.

May 29, 1912

Dear Marshal,
I hope you and Betty are doing well. We would really enjoy a visit. You both should come down and visit the ranch. You can stay in our guest house. I know it's hot here in the summertime, but we'll take good care of you. We'll take you out on the horses. How are the grandkids? I guess it's about time your grandson starts thinking about what he wants to do. He can always come down and work for me in Texas. He'd make a lot of money. The oil industry has been good to me and Martha. We've been drilling going on twelve years now. Our Peggy just had her third little girl. She and George live down the road from us. I reckon George will take over our family business soon. Martha and I would like to travel more to see the world while things are going good. You never know what might happen next.

Your friend, Old Man "i"

DIFFERENT PERSPECTIVES

Let's say that Marshal and his wife, Betty, did travel down to Texas to visit my grandparents. Write a story about them.

How did they get there? How long did it take? What was it like for people who lived up north to visit a ranch in Texas?

Write from either Marshal or Betty's perspective. Remember, they aren't used to the heat. They may have never been close to a horse. What do you think wealthy people lived like in Texas?

When Marshal and Betty arrived to Texas, they...

_____

_____

_____

_____

_____

_____

_____

_____

_____

_____

LET'T BRAINSTORM!

Use the space on the next two pages to write down a few things that interest you regarding some of the characters we just learned about. Be sure to list out some interesting problems too. You may even want to do a little more research on your own using your favorite character and his or her life. I wrote down all of the people we've discussed so far.

Cabeza de Vaca
Karankawas
Jane Hughs
Stephen F. Austin
Santa Anna
Sam Houston
Quanah Parker
Vivian White
Abraham Lincoln
Confederate Soldiers
Union
Infantry
Cavalry
General Robert E. Lee
General Ulysses S. Grant
Nurses
Cowboys
Ranchers
Charles Goodnight
Oliver Loving

After reading about so many inspirational people, I can't wait to write a story. Before we do, I'd love to get to know a little more about your history too! Let's start with where you were born. Can you **circle** it on one of the maps? In case you are an alien, I gave you a map of the solar system too.

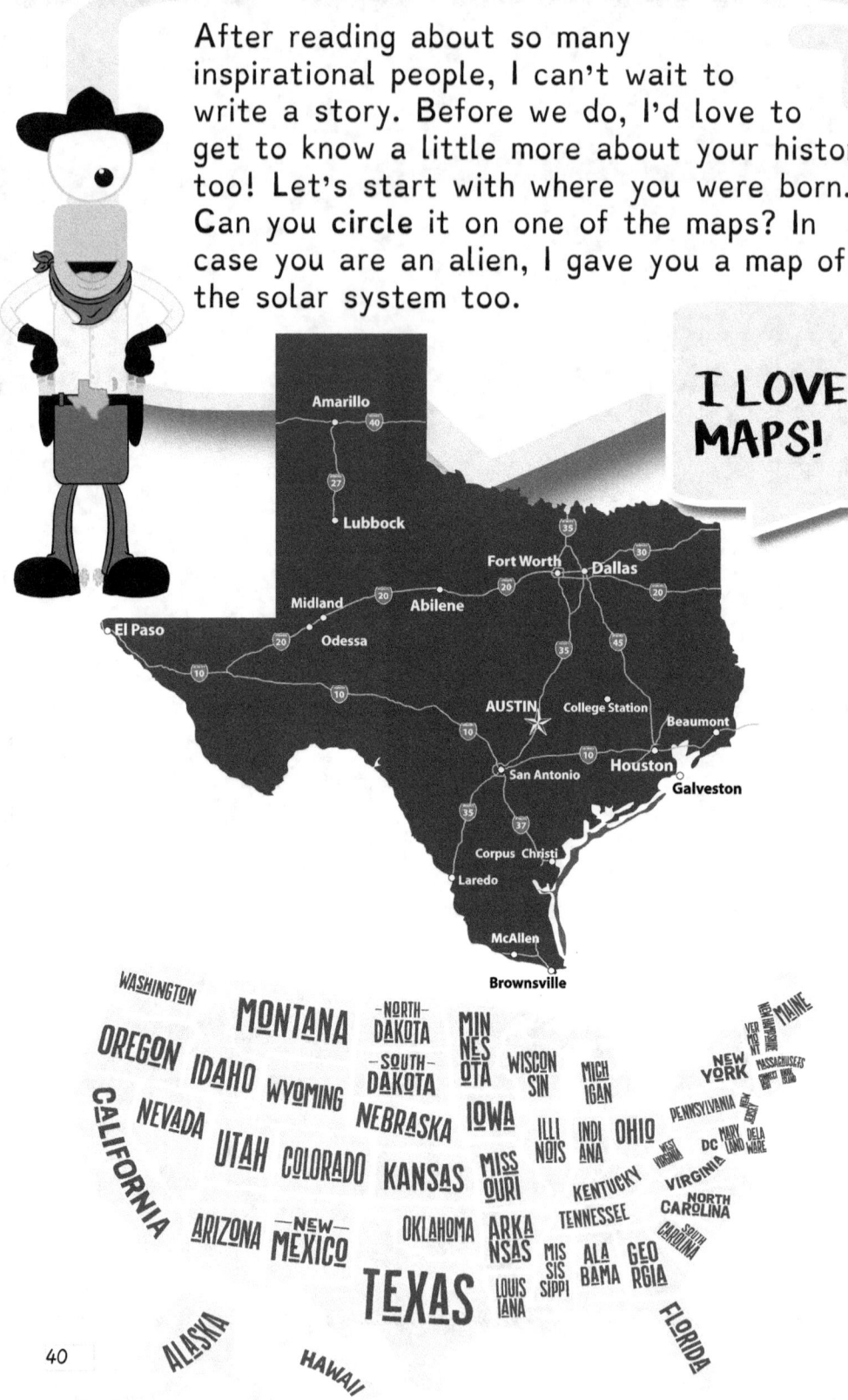

I LOVE MAPS!

Map of **The World**

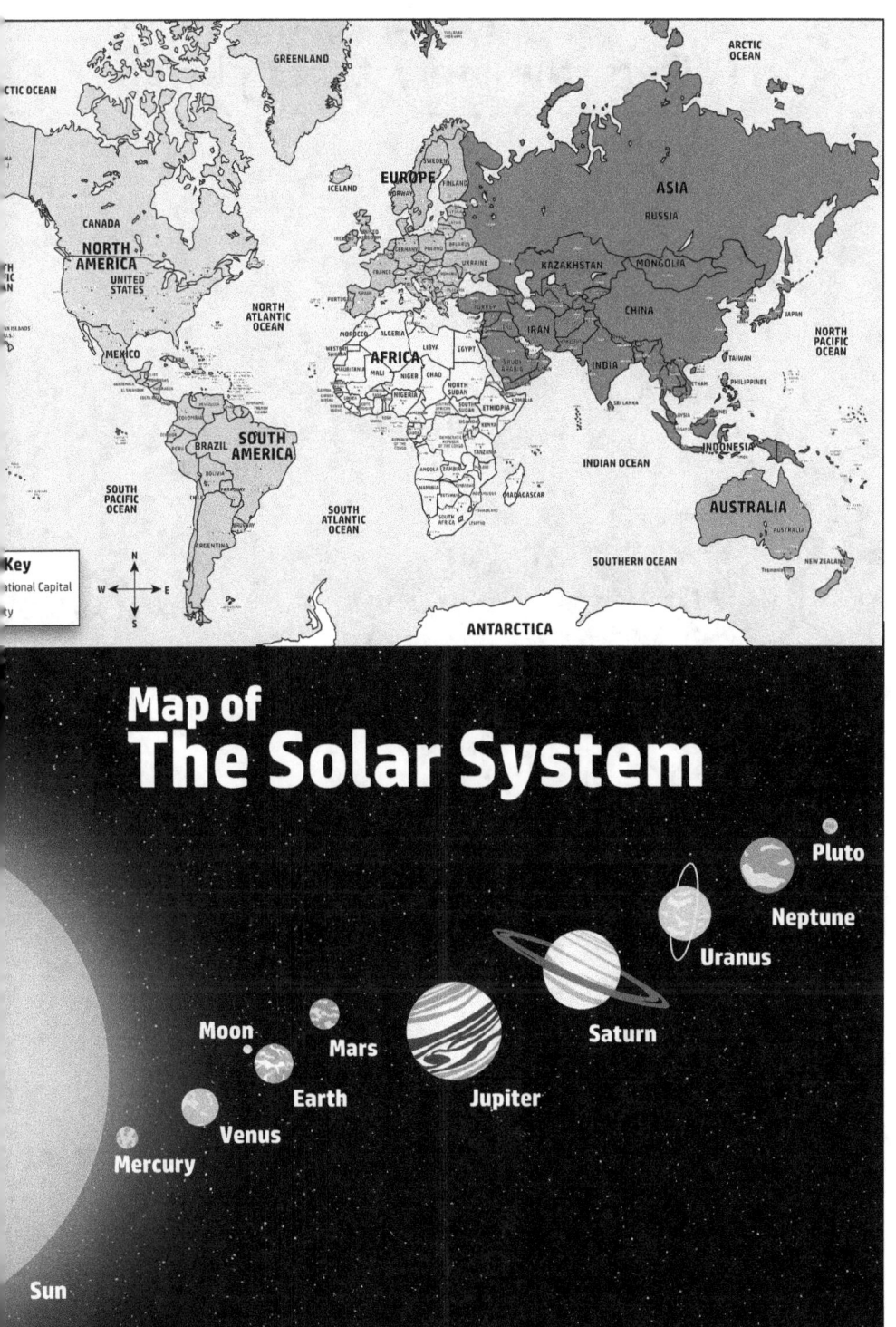

Map of **The Solar System**

SETTINGS

(Where the story takes place)

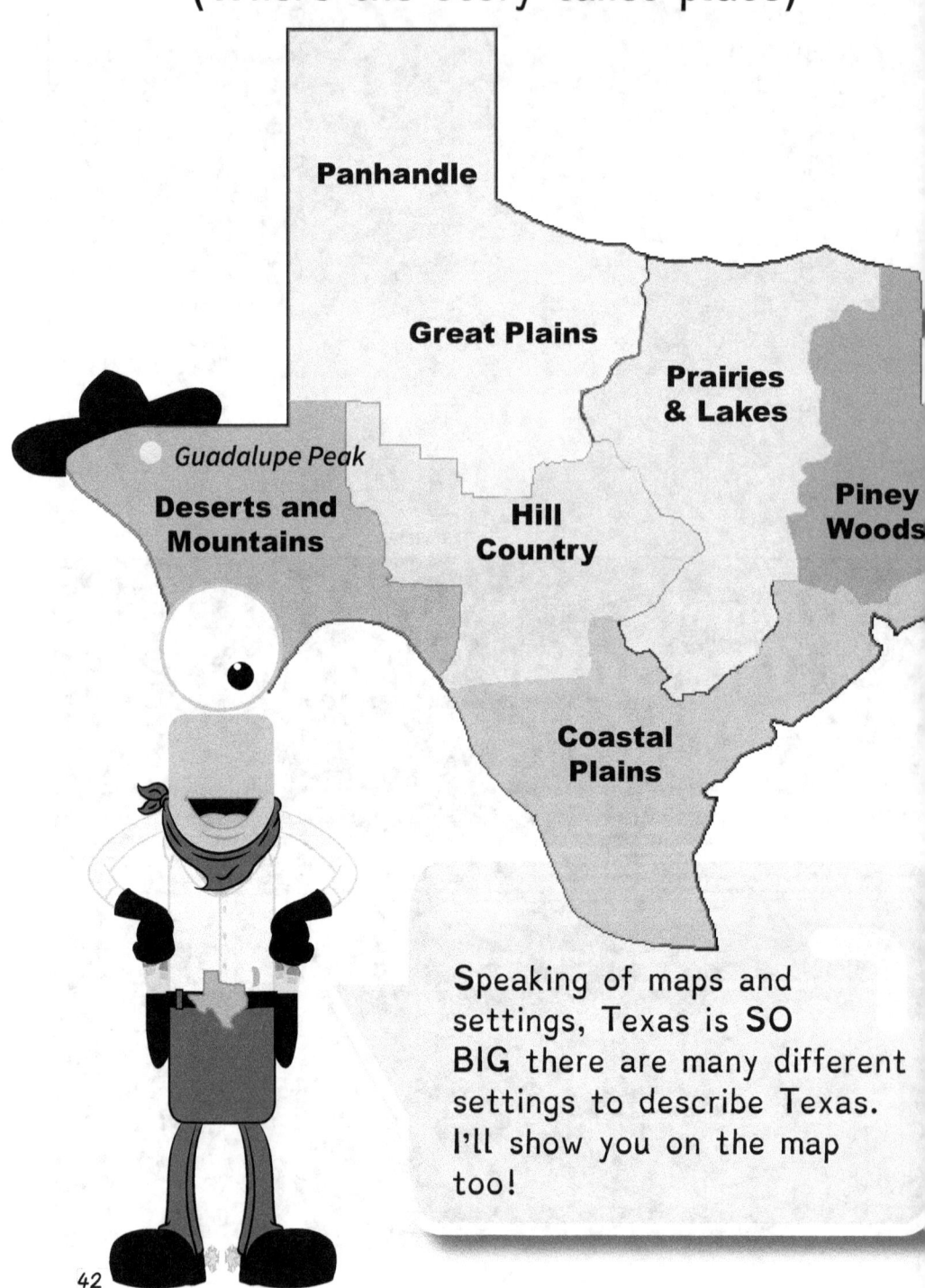

Panhandle

Great Plains

Prairies & Lakes

Guadalupe Peak

Deserts and Mountains

Hill Country

Piney Woods

Coastal Plains

Speaking of maps and settings, Texas is SO BIG there are many different settings to describe Texas. I'll show you on the map too!

Deserts and Mountains in the West. The tallest mountain in Texas is the Guadalupe Peak, at 8,750 feet, more than 1 1/2 miles above sea level.

Grasslands across the **Great Plains** and in the **Panhandle**. Grasslands can be flat and they can have hills too. This would be a great place for running ... or rolling my eyeball down a hill.

Texas also has Piney, Wooded Areas. There is a place in Texas called the **Piney Woods**. The trees are so tall there, they look like they touch the sky. I got to go on vacation to the Big Thicket when I was just old enough to blink. I got to see all kinds of trees, birds and wildlife when I visited. **Take a wild guess why people established towns near this area?**

_____

The answer is on the bottom of this page!

As you probably know, a large part of Texas literally sits on the **Gulf of Mexico**, so naturally we have all kinds of **Beach** and **Ocean** settings in the **Coastal Plains**. In these parts you will see more palm trees than pine trees due to the setting and climate.

ANSWER: LUMBER INDUSTRY   43

CLIMATE

Speaking of climate, Texas has all different kinds of weather patterns. It could be snowing in Dallas, raining in Galveston (where I live now) while the sun is out in Brownsville. Speaking of the sun ... Texas is one of the hottest states, especially in the summertime.

You'll want to think about all of these things when establishing the setting in your story soon. Also keep in mind how geography, environment and weather will affect your story characters.

Dallas

Galveston

Brownsville

I want you to think about your favorite character from Texas History. _____

Where did they live?_____

What was the climate like in that part of Texas?

_____

Go ahead and draw a map of Texas and mark the spot where he or she lived. If they had to travel, you may want to mark each spot and connect the dots.

Non-Fiction Facts about some of the first people in Texas

COMANCHE (Warriors)
- Lived on the Plains
- Skilled horsemen
- First to tame wild horses
- Hunted Bison
- Fought with settlers who tried to build houses on their land
- Disease killed many Comanche Indians in the 1800s

APACHE
- First lived on the Plains
- Enemies to the Comanche
- Set up camps in the Spring to grow vegetables
- Traveled to trade and hunt
- Defeated by the Comanche and had to move to the Mountains

THE USEFUL AND SACRED BISON:

- Yummy meat ... and tongue, liver, eyes, stomach, snout **AND BRAINS!**
- Hide for clothing, tipi covers, shields, pouches and winter robes!
- Bison horns for spoons
- Bison bones for knives
- Poop for fuel to start cooking fires!

KARANKAWA

- Lived along the Coast
- Nomads
- All of their resources came from the coastal land
- They used trees to build canoes
- They ate fish and shellfish

Let's Write a Story

47

BRAINSTORMING

We've been doing a lot of brainstorming for settings. Every time you research and learn something new, it's all a part of brainstorming ... especially if you are writing Historical Fiction. We will talk about the difference between Non-Fiction and Historical Fiction later. Let's play a game first!

Pick an animal and follow the arrows to see what your climate, setting and secondary character will be.

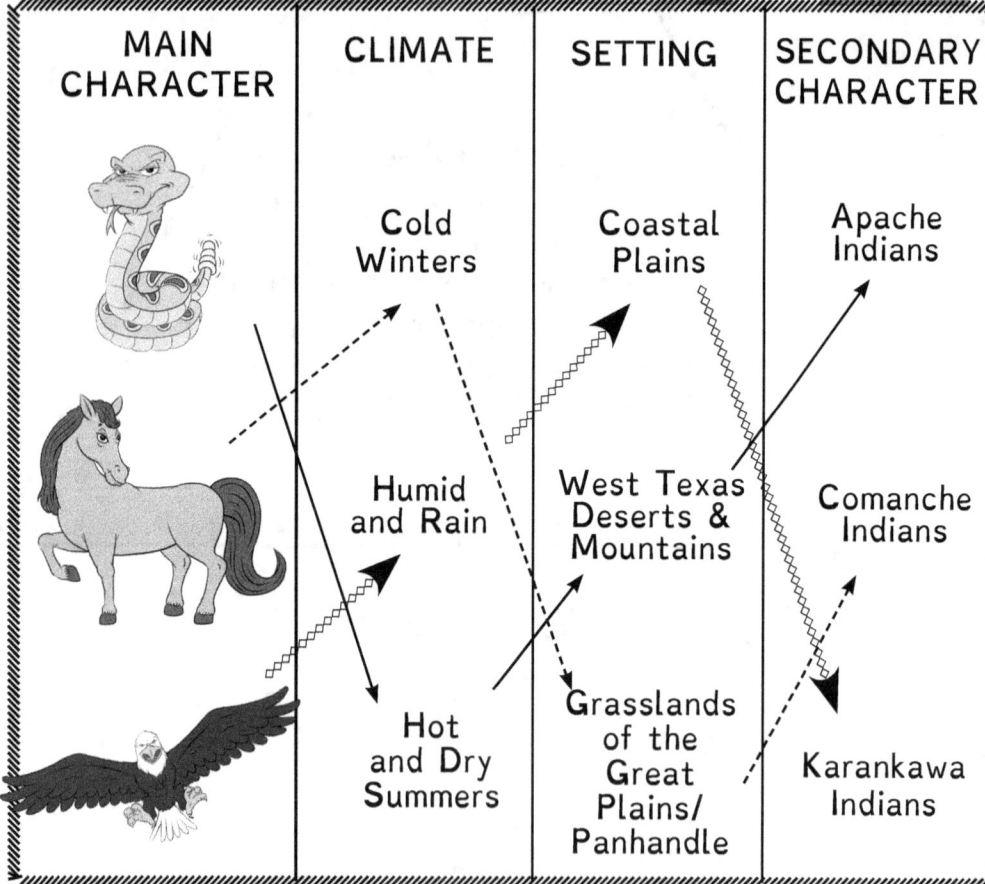

MAIN CHARACTER	CLIMATE	SETTING	SECONDARY CHARACTER
	Cold Winters	Coastal Plains	Apache Indians
	Humid and Rain	West Texas Deserts & Mountains	Comanche Indians
	Hot and Dry Summers	Grasslands of the Great Plains/ Panhandle	Karankawa Indians

Main Character _____

Climate _____

Setting: _____

Secondary Character _____

What is your character's problem? _____

_____

Let's write a story from the point of view of the animal you picked. They will be your main character in this story. Your animal will encounter a human in your story. That human could be a settler or even one of the natives.

Flip the page and write a short story! Be sure to include your animal, description of the climate, the setting and decide what kind of problem they will face or witness. What will your animal character do? Will they help the humans? Will they be afraid? Other problems could include the weather, lack of food, disease... don't forget about those too. Don't forget to use some of the facts I gave you from pages 46 & 47.

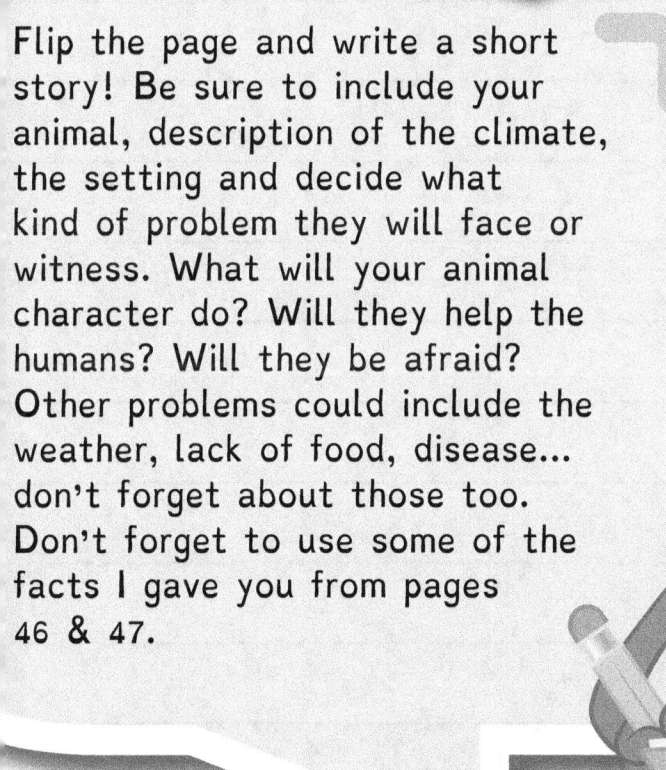

Write Your Story

Title _____

_____

_____

_____

_____

_____

_____

_____

_____

_____

_____

_____

_____

_____

_____

_____

_____

_____

_____

_____

You know, on some of the previous pages, I mentioned we would talk more about Non-Fiction and Historical Fiction writing. Soon we will be making up a Historical Fiction story together, but before we do let's go over the difference between the two.

Non-Fiction	Historical Fiction
When we **READ** and **WRITE** Non-Fiction that means we are writing down pure **FACTS** and **REAL EVENTS.** This type of writing is written about the **REAL LIVES OF PEOPLE.**	When we **READ** and **WRITE** Historical Fiction that means historical research has been used as inspiration. The plot takes place in a setting located in the past, but we still make up the story. The character doesn't have to be the exact character from a textbook, but the writer could use a real person's life for ideas in the story.
* Biographies * Autobiographies * Short Essays * Research Papers	* Number the Stars * Gone with the Wind * The Book Thief * Rango the movie

HISTORICAL FICTION

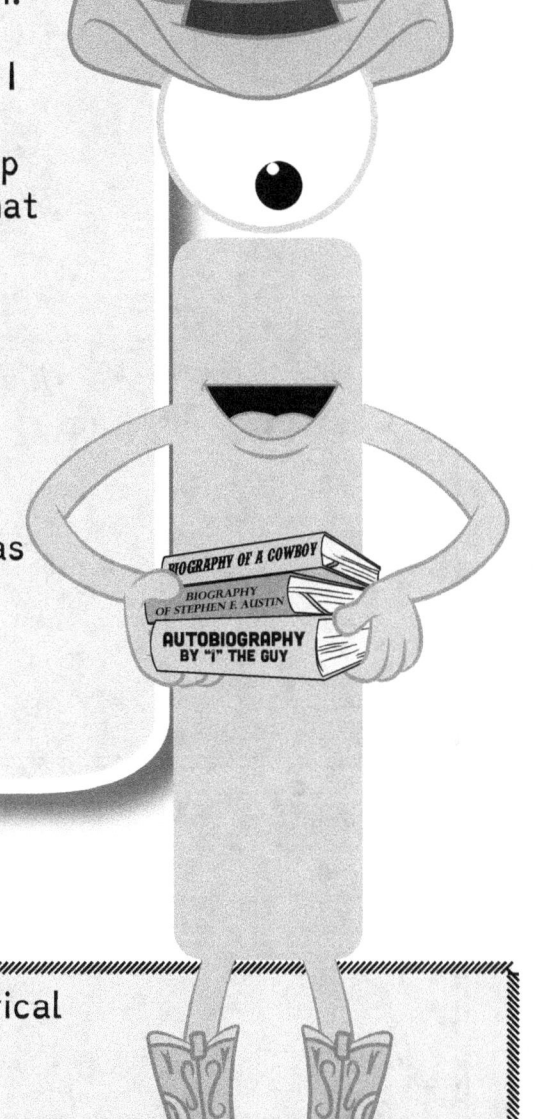

There are parts of this journal that are non-fiction. There are other parts of this journal where you and I might get inspired by some historical facts but make up a fun story about them. That would be called **Historical Fiction**.

My favorite examples of **Historical Fiction** can be found in some pretty awesome cartoons. Ever heard of Pecos Bill? He was a fictional cowboy whose adventures were based on expansion into the south.

Who is your favorite Historical Fiction character?

_____

CHARACTER

Let's do a character development chart for your favorite
Historical Fiction character.

Name/Character/Age	Setting
Qualities That Make This Character Different	Favorite Things
Strengths	Weakness

DEVELOPMENT

Family	Friends
Least Favorite Things	**Biggest Fear**
Prized Possession	**Physical Characteristics**

Once you start to come up with your own story character, you'll want to create a character chart for them too. Before we do, let's think about some ideas you would want to use in your own Historical Fiction Adventure. What would it be about? Feel free to write down a few things you may want to include in a story or things that you want to do more research on. I'll do an example with you.

"i" The Guy's Ideas

The Life of a Bison

Texas settings - Coastal / Beach

Texas when it was its own country

A Horse's Point of View

Santa Anna Plans

~~Kolaches~~

Rodeos

Cattle Drives

Oil Discovery

BRAINSTORMING BOX

REVIEW!!!!!

Hey! It's me again. "i" The Guy. So, let's just be clear here, I am a fictional character. Everything I tell you about myself was made up by the author who created me. When we READ and WRITE Fiction that means it is made up by using our imaginations.

BUT! Yes there's a BUT. We can still get inspired by real life and history to write FICTION.

I'll tell you a little bit about my HISTORY, since I'm basically the Main Character in my own story.

It's near the mountains and basins of Texas. Yes, Texas once had **HUGE** mountains. My great grandpa, Old Man "i", has passed down many stories to my family about our past. Come to find out, there were even **VOLCANOES** in Texas millions of years ago, only about twenty miles away from where I was born.

You may have noticed everything written down was a mixture of Non-Fiction facts about Texas, Fiction about me and Historical Fiction writing. Check out the key below to see which is which.

All of this together allows me to write Historical Fiction because it's inspired by real events, places and even people.

My story was first set in a little town in West Texas called Marfa. That's where my eyeball I was born. It's near the mountains and basins of Texas. Yes, Texas once had **HUGE** mountains millions of years ago. My great grandpa, Old Man "i", has passed down many stories to my family about our past. Come to find out, there were even **VOLCANOES** in Texas millions of years ago only about twenty miles away from where I was born.

KEY:

Non-Fiction   Fiction   Historical Fiction

TIME TRAVEL

Imagine you lived back in the late 1800s. That would be cool to go back there just for a day right? Pretend you are a settler moving to Texas. What part of Texas would you live and why? If you forget all the different parts of Texas, just flip a few pages back to get some ideas. (Page 42)

Write a short story about your move to Texas. It will be a Historical Fiction story. You will be the main character. Use what you've learned while making up your own action adventure!

I arrived to Texas...

_____

_____

_____

_____

_____

_____

_____

_____

POINT OF VIEW

You have had quite a few opportunities to write about other characters and even yourself as the main character in a story. Did you write in 1st Person Point of View or 3rd Person Point of View? Let's review the difference between the two.

1st Person POV
The Writer becomes the character in the story, so it sounds like the character is talking about themselves. The writer uses words like **I, me, we, us**. The reader gets to experience the story from the character's perspective.

3rd Person POV
The Writer writes about the character in the story, so it feels like the reader is watching the character do things. The writer uses words like **he, she, they** and the **name** of the character.

CIRCLE 1ST POV OR 3RD POV
FOR EACH OF THESE SENTENCES BELOW:

"i" The Guy ran
across the park
to find his eyeball.
1st   3rd

I saw a rattlesnake out of
the corner of my eye.
1st   3rd

My best friend is a cowboy.
1st   3rd

He traveled the Wild West
on the back of a horse.
1st   3rd

GALVESTON

Did you know Galveston is a **HUGE** part of Texas History?

I wanted to take a second to talk about Galveston, since that's where I live now.

Here are some facts!
- Galveston is along the Texas coast.
- Back in the late 1800s, Galveston was the largest Texas city!
- It was the busiest port for trade.
- The Great Storm of 1900 almost wiped Galveston off the map.
- The Great Storm was the deadliest natural disaster in U.S. history and forever changed Galveston.
- The island was raised up about 18 feet.

Some of the buildings weren't completely destroyed by the Great Storm. One of those buildings was the Orphanage on 21st Street. Today it is the home to a Texas history museum.

Do you know what it is called?

(Answer: The Bryan Museum)

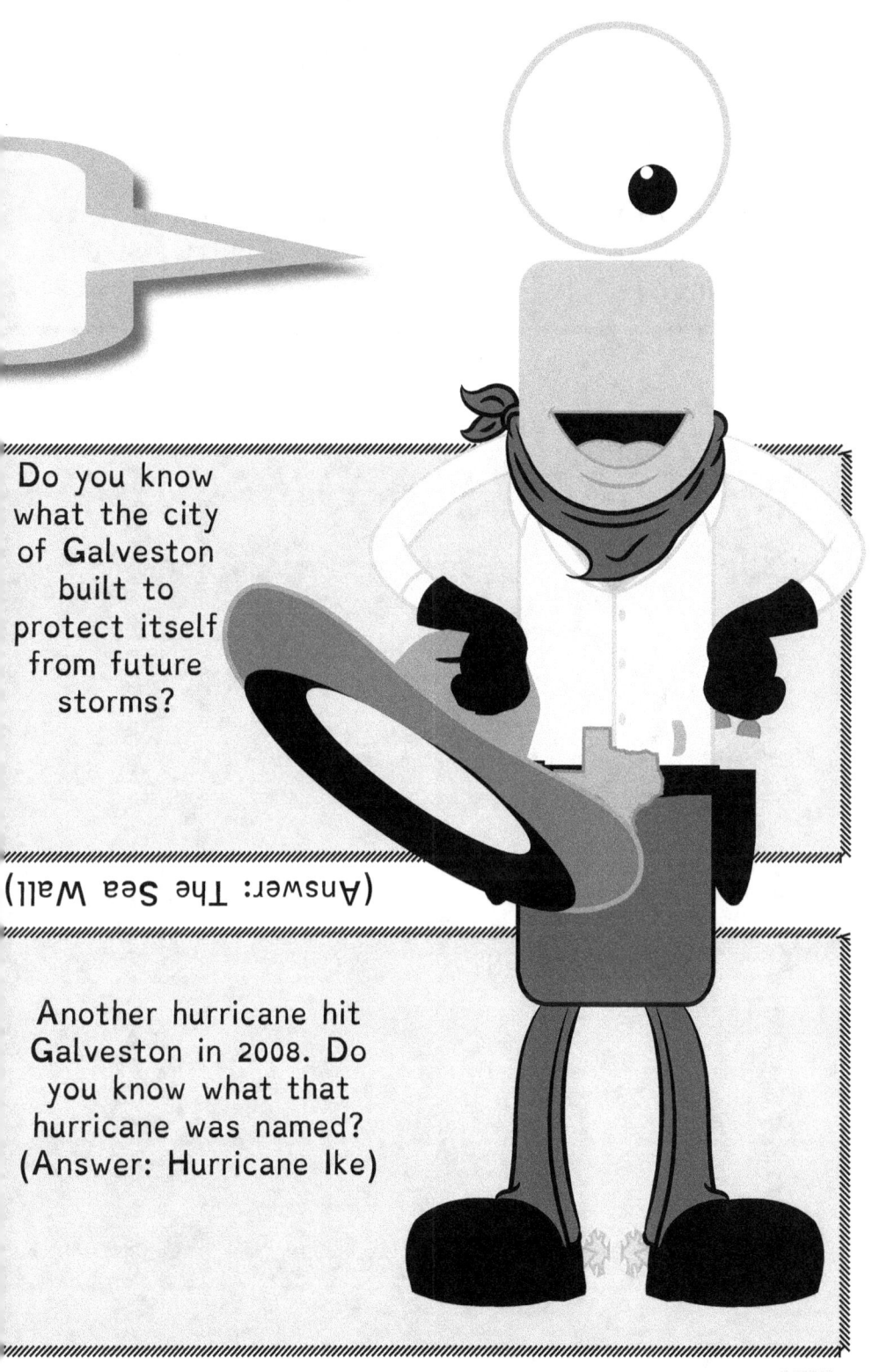

Do you know what the city of **Galveston** built to protect itself from future storms?

(Answer: The Sea Wall)

Another hurricane hit Galveston in 2008. Do you know what that hurricane was named? (Answer: Hurricane Ike)

IMAGINE

Imagine you lived through the Great Storm of 1900. What would it be like to be hit by a hurricane with no warning?

What would you feel?

What thoughts would be racing through your head?

What would you do?

What would the scene look like?
Describe it first, then draw it.

_____

_____

_____

_____

_____

_____

_____

_____

TIME TRAVEL

Imagine you are a resident of Galveston back in 1900. Maybe you were sitting inside your home or outside when the storm clouds rolled in. Write a story of the experience and what you did to survive. Remember, this is a Historical Fiction story because you are making it up but using parts of real history for inspiration.

_____

_____

_____

_____

_____

_____

_____

_____

_____

_____

_____

_____

We've been learning **A LOT** about Texas and the people who put Texas on the map! There are so many stories inside the history of Texas. Now it's time for you to write a historical fiction story. Feel free to use what we've learned so far for inspiration.

Let's go ahead and outline the important things we'll need to consider for our story.

MAIN CHARACTER

Name: _____

Age or year of birth: _____

Physical Description: _____

_____

Favorite Things: _____

_____

Personality Characteristics: _____

_____

Sketch the Character

Most Prized Possession: _____

_____

Favorite Activity: _____

_____

Biggest Fear: _____

_____

Strengths: _____

_____

Weakness: _____

_____

Is there anyone from history who has inspired the development of your character?

_____

SETTING

Name of the place

Time Period

Climate

Description of the setting

Draw the Setting

SECONDARY CHARACTERS

These characters help the main character **(HERO)** and sometimes even cause a problem for the Hero.

The Sidekick(s):

Sidekicks are allies to the Hero. That means they are friends. Sidekicks are funny and present a comic element to the story. Sidekicks are good for helping the Hero out, especially if they are in trouble. Villains tend to have sidekicks too.

The Mentor:

The Mentor is usually an older or wiser character. Mentors are good teachers or coaches for the Hero. Mentors help the Hero in their times of need. Mentors share their wisdom and sometimes secrets to help the Hero change in the story.

The Villain:

The Villain is the Antagonist. This means a villain is the bad guy or girl. Villains are usually just as smart or strong as the Hero. Villains are a challenge for the Hero. Villains represent a conflict or problem in the story. Villains also have flaws and weaknesses.

Who could be your hero's sidekick?

Who could be your hero's mentor?

Who could be your hero's villain?

SECONDARY CHARACTERS

List at least 3 things to describe the other characters in the story. Consider names, appearance and special skills.

Side Kick(s)

Mentor

Villain

Others

PROBLEM

Is your character's problem internal or external?

Brainstorm a few potential problems your character could encounter.

CLIMAX

The climax is the most intense part of the story, found toward the end. Start thinking about a good climax for your story so your readers will stay on the edge of their seats. You can fill in this box later.

RESOLUTION (SOLUTION)

One thing I like to remind all writers is: DO NOT FIX YOUR CHARACTER'S PROBLEM TOO SOON! Problems will lead to even more problems, so be sure to take time to develop your character's problem and even allow them to fail a time or two before you fix it.

Feel free to brainstorm a few potential ideas for your story resolution.

STORY OUTLINE

Are you ready to learn the way real writers outline their stories? Many of them don't have super structured ways of making a perfect outline. They literally write all the things they want to happen in their story, in no particular order, so they don't forget. Go ahead and give it a try. I wrote an example of my own on page 84. The whole point is so you don't forget some of your good ideas in the middle of your writing.

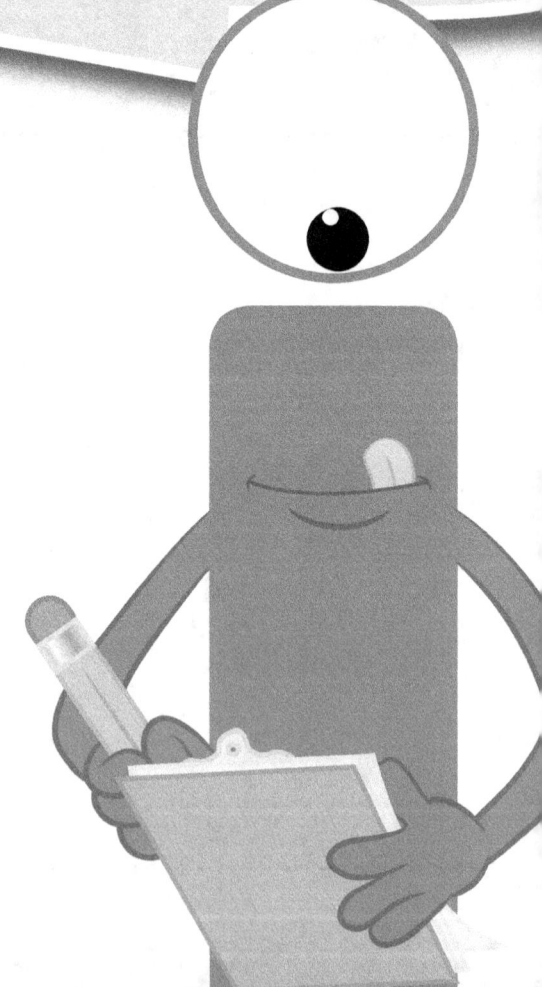

"i" The Guy's example Story Outline

Possible Titles: The Oil Cowboy ???

From the perspective of a cowboy on the trail

forgotten cowboys - what did cowboys do for work after the cattle boom ended

Character Name - Charley Baker

Backstory to trickle into the story: Born in Pasadena, Father (a cowboy) passed away when Charley was 17, so he had to take care of mama and sister.....

Started as a cowboy for work when he was 18 years old, even though many towns didn't allow cattle to pass through anymore

'''' Horse's name was ~~Bob~~ Hairy.

He always had a book in his saddle - would read every night before going to bed on the trail

...Once we was confronted by Native Americans on one of his cattle drives while he was resting / He gave them the pocket knife his Pa gave him so they would leave him alone and not steal his horse

** He considered a new profession and ~~thought~~ decided he should at least head back south to his mom and sister **

(He can share some of this backstory in conversations with his wife or kids in the story to get to know him better.)

This is where the story really starts: Charley read that guys were trying to find oil in Texas

He knew there was opportunity in Texas. He knew he had to go back to Texas and just believe.

He married a girl he met in Pasadena, Mary.

Her dad was drilling for oil, so he went to go work for him..........

They would find some oil, but not too much in the beginning. They had 2 kids. Boy and Girl (David and Ann) They were poor. **Describe what all they had and what they had to eat. Bread and beans. His daughter would always bring home a stray dog. She loved animals.

Problem: He could never find a job for a long amount of time.

Charley and his family moved to Galveston - 1897 - New Job - Digging water wells along the railroad tracks. They brought their dog, Buck Boy.

Climax of story: 1900 - Deadliest Storm hits Galveston. They lost everything, even their dog. Describe the scene. They even thought they lost one of their daughter, Ann, but she was searching for Buck Boy. Describe what they lost.

1901 - Oil was found at Spindletop. Lot's of oil. They moved the family to Beaumont. Right before they left, they found Buck. They had to take a train. Charley got back in the drilling business and made a life for him and his family.

Three Act Structure

Stories are always divided into three acts. The <u>BEGINNING</u> includes the character, setting and the reason for the character's problem. The <u>MIDDLE</u> section is where the action of the story happens. The problems tend to get bigger at this point. This is where you should add in your other characters to help or cause conflict. At the end of the Middle, the most exciting part of the story emerges, the climax. The <u>END</u> of the story includes the resolution and the lesson is learned. This is where we can see that the character has changed. Now it's time to put your story ideas in order on the next page.

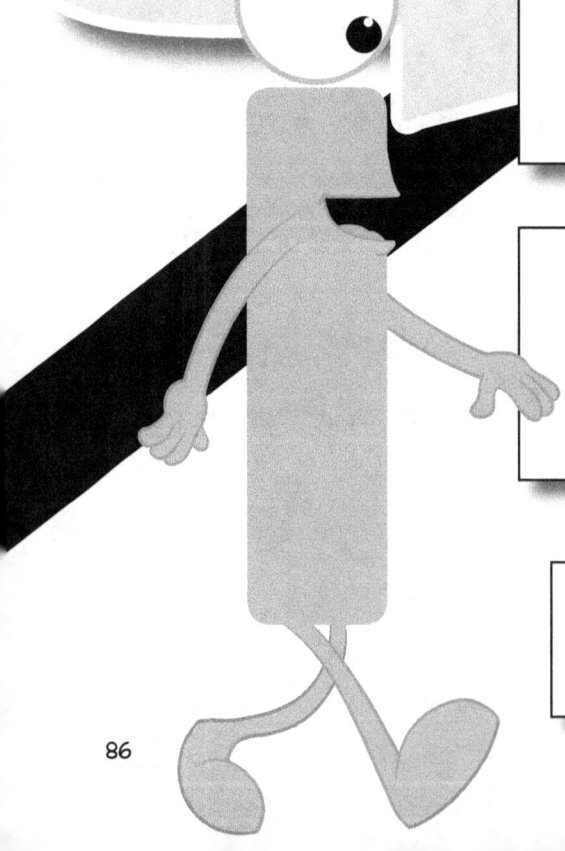

Conflict

The character's problems that they are trying to overcome.

Climax

The **BIG** finish. The story is over after the climax. Remember, this happens at the very end of Act 2.

Resolution

The way the character solves the problem.

Beginning: Act I (Introduction)

Middle: Act 2 (Development)

End: Act 3 (Resolution)

WAYS TO START YOUR STORY

You've got a ton of brainstorming notes. Now it's time to start. If you can't think of a way to start your story, pick up a few books to see how other authors do it. There are so many different ways to start. Remember this is just a rough draft. It's not going to be perfect.

Dialogue

Dive into Action

Shock the Reader

Interesting Narrator Voice

Introduce the Character

Visually describe the setting

Pivotal moment

OR Just Start! You can go back later.

START YOUR ROUGH DRAFT HERE

"i" THE GUY'S
HISTORY RESOURCE SECTION

THE BRYAN MUSEUM

The Texas Declaration of Independence
March 2, 1836

When a government has ceased to protect the lives, liberty and property of the people, from whom its legitimate powers are derived, and for the advancement of whose happiness it was instituted, and so far from being a guarantee for the enjoyment of those inestimable and inalienable rights, becomes an instrument in the hands of evil rulers for their oppression.

When the Federal Republican Constitution of their country, which they have sworn to support, no longer has a substantial existence, and the whole nature of their government has been forcibly changed, without their consent, from a restricted federative republic, composed of sovereign states, to a consolidated central military despotism, in which every interest is disregarded but that of the army and the priesthood, both the eternal enemies of civil liberty, the everready minions of power, and the usual instruments of tyrants.

When, long after the spirit of the constitution has departed, moderation is at length so far lost by those in power, that even the semblance of freedom is removed, and the forms themselves of the constitution discontinued, and so far from their petitions and remonstrances being regarded, the agents who bear them are thrown into dungeons, and mercenary armies sent forth to force a new government upon them at the point of the bayonet.

When, in consequence of such acts of malfeasance and abdication on the part of the government, anarchy prevails, and civil society is dissolved into its original elements. In such a crisis, the first law of nature, the right of self-preservation, the inherent and inalienable rights of the people to appeal to first principles, and take their political affairs into their own hands in extreme cases, enjoins it as a right towards themselves, and a sacred obligation to their posterity, to abolish such government, and create another in its stead, calculated to rescue them from impending dangers, and to secure their future welfare and happiness.

Nations, as well as individuals, are amenable for their acts to the public opinion of mankind. A statement of a part of our grievances is therefore submitted to an impartial world, in justification of the hazardous but unavoidable step now taken, of severing our political connection with the Mexican people, and assuming an independent attitude among the nations of the earth.

The Mexican government, by its colonization laws, invited and induced the Anglo-American population of Texas to colonize its wilderness under the pledged faith of a written constitution, that they should continue to enjoy that constitutional liberty and republican government to which they had been habituated in the land of their birth, the United States of America.

In this expectation they have been cruelly disappointed, inasmuch as the Mexican nation has acquiesced in the late changes made in the government by General Antonio Lopez de Santa Anna, who having overturned the constitution of his country, now offers us the cruel alternative, either to abandon our homes, acquired by so many privations, or submit to the most intolerable of all tyranny, the combined despotism of the sword and the priesthood.

It has sacrificed our welfare to the state of Coahuila, by which our interests have been continually depressed through a jealous and partial course of legislation, carried on at a far distant seat of government, by a hostile majority, in an unknown tongue, and this too, notwithstanding we have petitioned in the humblest terms for the establishment of a separate state government, and have, in accordance with the provisions of the national constitution, presented to the general Congress a republican constitution, which was, without just cause, contemptuously rejected.

It incarcerated in a dungeon, for a long time, one of our citizens, for no other cause but a zealous endeavor to procure the acceptance of our constitution, and the establishment of a state government.

It has failed and refused to secure, on a firm basis, the right of trial by jury, that palladium of civil liberty, and only safe guarantee for the life, liberty, and property of the citizen.

It has failed to establish any public system of education, although possessed of almost boundless resources, (the public domain,) and although it is an axiom in political science, that unless a people are educated and enlightened, it is idle to expect the continuance of civil liberty, or the capacity for self government.

It has suffered the military commandants, stationed among us, to exercise arbitrary acts of oppression and tyrrany, thus trampling upon the most sacred rights of the citizens, and rendering the military superior to the civil power.

It has dissolved, by force of arms, the state Congress of Coahuila and Texas, and obliged our representatives to fly for their lives from the seat of government, thus depriving us of the fundamental political right of representation.

It has demanded the surrender of a number of our citizens, and ordered military detachments to seize and carry them into the Interior for trial, in contempt of the civil authorities, and in defiance of the laws and the constitution.

It has made piratical attacks upon our commerce, by commissioning foreign desperadoes, and authorizing them to seize our vessels, and convey the property of our citizens to far distant ports for confiscation.

It denies us the right of worshipping the Almighty according to the dictates of our own conscience, by the support of a national religion, calculated to promote the temporal interest of its human functionaries, rather than the glory of the true and living God.

It has demanded us to deliver up our arms, which are essential to our defence, the rightful property of freemen, and formidable only to tyrannical governments.

It has invaded our country both by sea and by land, with intent to lay waste our territory, and drive us from our homes; and has now a large mercenary army advancing, to carry on against us a war of extermination.

It has, through its emissaries, incited the merciless savage, with the tomahawk and scalping knife, to massacre the inhabitants of our defenseless frontiers.

It hath been, during the whole time of our connection with it, the contemptible sport and victim of successive military revolutions, and hath continually exhibited every characteristic of a weak, corrupt, and tyrranical government.

These, and other grievances, were patiently borne by the people of Texas, untill they reached that point at which forbearance ceases to be a virtue. We then took up arms in defence of the national constitution. We appealed to our Mexican brethren for assistance. Our appeal has been made in vain. Though months have elapsed, no sympathetic response has yet been heard from the Interior.

We are, therefore, forced to the melancholy conclusion, that the Mexican people have acquiesced in the destruction of their liberty, and the substitution therfor of a military government; that they are unfit to be free, and incapable of self government.

The necessity of self-preservation, therefore, now decrees our eternal political separation.

We, therefore, the delegates with plenary powers of the people of Texas, in solemn convention assembled, appealing to a candid world for the necessities of our condition, do hereby resolve and declare, that our political connection with the Mexican nation has forever ended, and that the people of Texas do now constitute a free, Sovereign, and independent republic, and are fully invested with all the rights and attributes which properly belong to independent nations; and, conscious of the rectitude of our intentions, we fearlessly and confidently commit the issue to the decision of the Supreme arbiter of the destinies of nations.

[Signed, in the order shown on the handwritten document]

John S. D. Byrom	Thomas Jefferson Rusk
Francis Ruis	Chas. S. Taylor
J. Antonio Navarro	John S. Roberts
Jesse B. Badgett	Robert Hamilton
Wm D. Lacy	Collin McKinney
William Menifee	Albert H. Latimer
Jn. Fisher	James Power
Matthew Caldwell	Sam Houston
William Motley	David Thomas
Lorenzo de Zavala	Edwd. Conrad
Stephen H. Everett	Martin Parmer
George W. Smyth	Edwin O. Legrand
Elijah Stapp	Stephen W. Blount
Claiborne West	Jms. Gaines
Wm. B. Scates	Wm. Clark, Jr.
M. B. Menard	Sydney O. Pennington
A. B. Hardin	Wm. Carrol Crawford
J. W. Bunton	Jno. Turner
Thos. J. Gazley	Benj. Briggs Goodrich
R. M. Coleman	G. W. Barnett
Sterling C. Robertson	James G. Swisher
Richard Ellis, *President of the Convention and Delegate from Red River*	Jesse Grimes
	S. Rhoads Fisher
James Collinsworth	John W. Moore
Edwin Waller	John W. Bower
Asa Brigham	Saml. A. Maverick *(from Bejar)*
Charles B. Stewart	Sam P. Carson
Thomas Barnett	A. Briscoe
Geo. C. Childress	J. B. Woods
Bailey Hardeman	H. S. Kimble, Secretary
Rob. Potter	

The Emancipation Proclamation, January 1, 1863

A Proclamation.

Whereas, on the twenty-second day of September, in the year of our Lord one thousand eight hundred and sixty-two, a proclamation was issued by the President of the United States, containing, among other things, the following, to wit:

"That on the first day of January, in the year of our Lord one thousand eight hundred and sixty-three, all persons held as slaves within any State or designated part of a State, the people whereof shall then be in rebellion against the United States, shall be then, thenceforward, and forever free; and the Executive Government of the United States, including the military and naval authority thereof, will recognize and maintain the freedom of such persons, and will do no act or acts to repress such persons, or any of them, in any efforts they may make for their actual freedom.

"That the Executive will, on the first day of January aforesaid, by proclamation, designate the States and parts of States, if any, in which the people thereof, respectively, shall then be in rebellion against the United States; and the fact that any State, or the people thereof, shall on that day be, in good faith, represented in the Congress of the United States by members chosen thereto at elections wherein a majority of the qualified voters of such State shall have participated, shall, in the absence of strong countervailing testimony, be deemed conclusive evidence that such State, and the people thereof, are not then in rebellion against the United States."

Now, therefore I, Abraham Lincoln, President of the United States, by virtue of the power in me vested as Commander-in-Chief, of the Army and Navy of the United States in time of actual armed rebellion against the authority and government of the United States, and as a fit and necessary war measure for suppressing said rebellion, do, on this first day of January, in the year of our Lord one thousand eight hundred and sixty-three, and in accordance with my purpose so to do publicly proclaimed for the full period of one hundred days, from the day first above mentioned, order and designate as the States and parts of States wherein the people thereof respectively, are this day in rebellion against the United States, the following, to wit:
Arkansas, Texas, Louisiana, (except the Parishes of St. Bernard, Plaquemines, Jefferson, St. John, St. Charles, St. James Ascension, Assumption, Terrebonne, Lafourche, St. Mary, St. Martin, and Orleans, including the City of New Orleans) Mississippi, Alabama, Florida, Georgia, South Carolina, North Carolina, and Virginia, (except the forty-eight counties designated as West Virginia, and also the counties of Berkley, Accomac, Northampton, Elizabeth City, York, Princess Ann, and Norfolk, including the cities of Norfolk and Portsmouth[)], and which excepted parts, are for the present, left precisely as if this proclamation were not issued.

And by virtue of the power, and for the purpose aforesaid, I do order and declare that all persons held as slaves within said designated States, and parts of States, are, and henceforward shall be free; and that the Executive government of the United States, including the military and naval authorities thereof, will recognize and maintain the freedom of said persons.

And I hereby enjoin upon the people so declared to be free to abstain from all violence, unless in necessary self-defence; and I recommend to them that, in all cases when allowed, they labor faithfully for reasonable wages.

And I further declare and make known, that such persons of suitable condition, will be received into the armed service of the United States to garrison forts, positions, stations, and other places, and to man vessels of all sorts in said service.

And upon this act, sincerely believed to be an act of justice, warranted by the Constitution, upon military necessity, I invoke the considerate judgment of mankind, and the gracious favor of Almighty God.

In witness whereof, I have hereunto set my hand and caused the seal of the United States to be affixed.

Done at the City of Washington, this first day of January, in the year of our Lord one thousand eight hundred and sixty three, and of the Independence of the United States of America the eighty-seventh.

By the President: *ABRAHAM LINCOLN*
WILLIAM H. SEWARD, Secretary of State.

Cattle Drive Map

Cowboy Gear

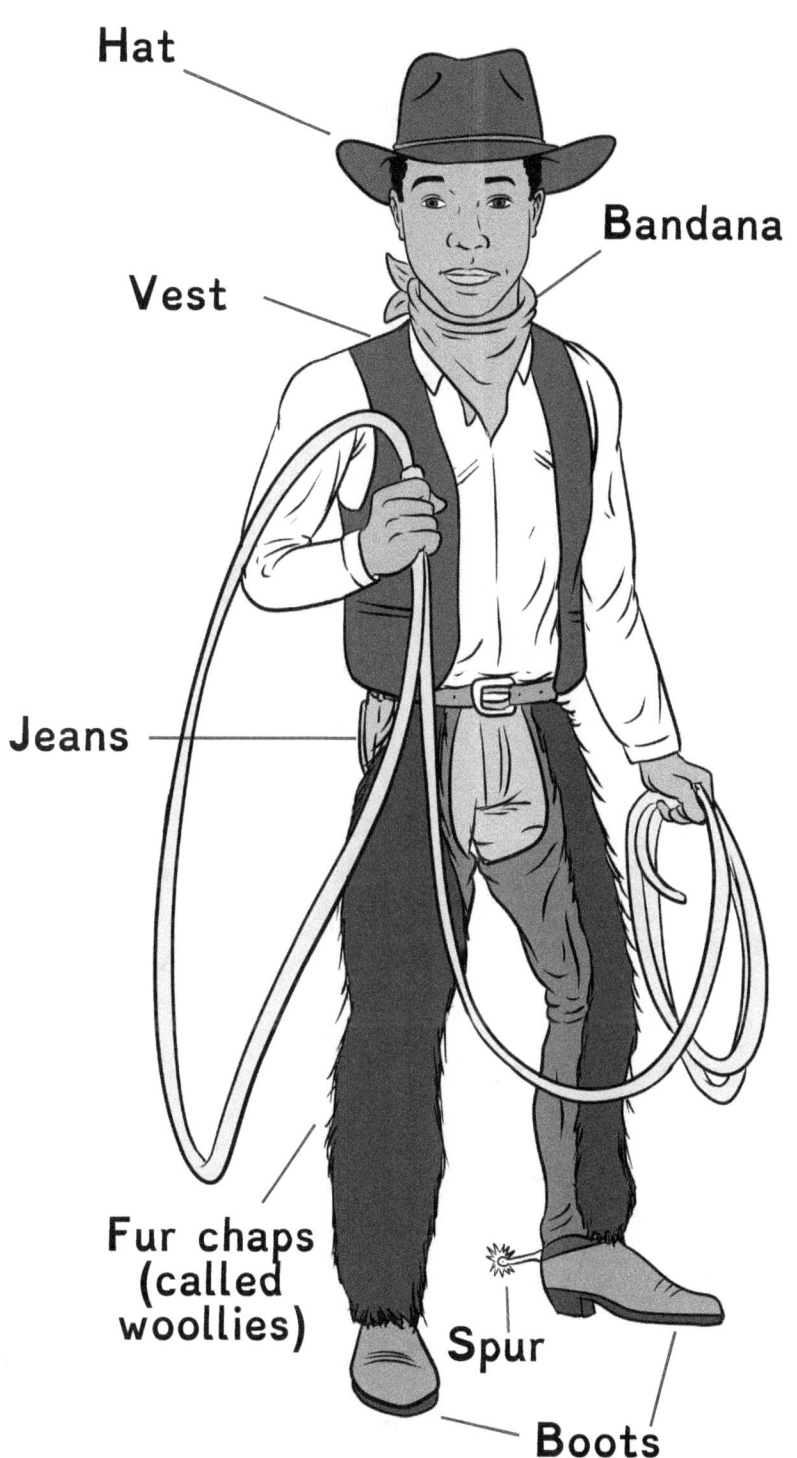

Hat

Bandana

Vest

Jeans

Fur chaps (called woollies)

Spur

Boots

www.ingramcontent.com/pod-product-compliance
Lightning Source LLC
Chambersburg PA
CBHW070342130626
46556CB00007B/2987